ENDANGERED!

DOLPHINS

Johannah Haney

Marshall Cavendish
Benchmark
New York

Marshall Cavendish Benchmark
99 White Plains Road
Tarrytown, New York 10591
www.marshallcavendish.us

Editor: Peter Mavrikis
Publisher: Michelle Bisson
Art Director: Anahid Hamparian
Series Designer: Elynn Cohen
Cover Design by Kay Petronio

Library of Congress Cataloging-in-Publication Data

Haney, Johannah.
Dolphins / by Johannah Haney.
p. cm. — (Endangered!)
Includes bibliographical references and index.
Summary: "Describes the characteristics, behavior, and plight of
endangered dolphins, and what people can do to help"—Provided by publisher.
ISBN 978-0-7614-4049-9
1. Dolphins—Juvenile literature. 2. Endangered species—Juvenile
literature. I. Title.
QL737.C432H366 2011
599.53—dc22
2009020334

Front cover: Bottlenose dolphin
Title page: Dolphins breaching
Back cover: Bottlenose and Risso dolphin (top); Pantropical Spotted dolphin (bottom)
Photo research by Paulee Kestin
Front cover: Lawrence Migdale / Photo Researchers, Inc.

The photographs in this book are used by permission and through the courtesy of:
Animals Animals: title page. *Ardea*: Augusto Stanzani, 4, 15, back cover (top); Francois Gohier, 6, 19,
M. Watson, 26; Nick Gordon, 28. *Getty Images*: Stockbyte, 7; Jeff Rotman, 14. *Peter Arnold*: Gerard Lacz, 9, 20;
Jonathan Bird, 10; Biosphere, 24; M.&C.DENIS-HUOT, 35. *Rotman*: 11, 16, 35. *Corbis*: Kennan Ward, 12;
Joerg Carstensen, 17; Bettmann, 41; Andy Rain, 43. *Minden Pictures*: Hiroya Minakuchi, 22,
back cover (bottom); Todd Pusser, 30. *AP Images*: Chris O'Meara, 36, 40; Oscar Sosa, 38.

Printed in Malaysia (T)
1 2 3 4 5 6

Contents

1

Intelligent Dolphins

A smooth, graceful dolphin arcs over the waves, her young **calf** right by her side. Together they dive into the depths in search of fish, then break out over the waves to take a breath, exhaling through their **blowholes** as they reach the surface. When they have finished eating, they might play some games, such as blowing a tower of swirling bubbles and swimming up through the middle. They might also signal to the other members of their

This dolphin is exhaling through its blowhole, creating a tower of bubbles in the water.

pod—the group of dolphins they swim with—by leaping through the air and landing with a great splash.

Dolphin behavior is fascinating and can be a lot fun to watch. But sadly, some types of dolphins have become **endangered**. Endangered animals are dying faster than young animals are born to replace them. Sometimes pollution makes it difficult or impossible for a **species**, or a specific type of animal, to continue living in its natural **habitat**. Other times, humans hunt the animals so much

Several dolphin pods traveling together.

This dolphin is trapped in a fishnet.

that they cannot reproduce fast enough to replace their lost individuals. A common disaster for marine mammals like dolphins is that they may get trapped in fishnets, even if the nets are meant to catch fish.

MARINE MAMMALS

Dolphins are marine mammals. That means that they live in water but must breathe air, they give birth to live young, and they nurse their offspring with milk. Dolphins are **cetaceans** and belong to a scientific grouping of animals that includes marine mammals such as whales and **porpoises**.

Different dolphin species grow to be various sizes. The smallest dolphin is the endangered Maui's dolphin, which grows to be 4 to 5 feet (1.2 to 1.5 meters) long and to weigh about 75 to 110 pounds (34 to 50 kilograms). The largest member of the dolphin family is the orca, commonly known as the killer whale. Male killer whales can grow to be about 20 feet (6 m) long and to weigh about 6.5 tons (5.9 tonnes).

Dolphins fish for their food, which includes squid, shrimp, and many types of fish. Most dolphins eat about 5 percent of their body weight in food each day. So if a dolphin weighs 250 pounds (113 kg), it will normally eat about 12.5 pounds (5.7 kg) of food every day.

Dolphins are very social animals, and they swim together in groups called pods. A pod of dolphins usually has twelve to twenty-four members. Dolphins form close bonds with the other members of their pods and will help a sick or injured member of their pod.

Sometimes dolphins will change to a new pod. Other

Orca whales can eat as much as 500 pounds (227 kg) of food each day, and they can swim as fast as 30 miles (48 km) per hour.

times, a number of pods will join together and form a **superpod** with hundreds—or even thousands—of dolphins. Dolphins benefit from being in pods because they can help each other. But swimming in pods can also make dolphins a target. Fishermen look for pods of dolphins because they know that tuna—a favorite food for dolphins—will be nearby. Being so easy to find puts dolphins in danger of being caught in the tuna nets.

DOLPHIN INTELLIGENCE

Scientists believe dolphins are among the most intelligent animals. One reason for that is because dolphins play complex games. One such game involves blowing tubes of bubbles into the water, then swimming and playing inside the bubbles. Dolphins also seem to enjoy playing in the waves created by passing boats, allowing the force of waves to pull the dolphin along on a fast ride. These types of playful behaviors are signs of advanced intelligence.

Scientists believe the complex and creative games that dolphins play help them learn about their environment.

DOLPHIN-HUMAN INTERACTION

Many humans feel a special connection to dolphins. Their natural intelligence, along with their playfulness, draws humans to dolphins. This has helped dolphins because a lot of humans want to protect them and their environment. It can also place dolphins at risk, however. Dolphins are sometimes killed as hunters try to capture dolphins to sell to marine parks. Curious humans in boats can put dolphins in danger of being injured by the boat's propeller.

Humans often feel a special bond with dolphins, but even friendly interactions like this put dolphins at risk.

2

Dolphin Facts

Dolphins swim great distances, sometimes as far as 100 miles (161 km) each day. Dolphins' bodies are shaped to help them swim easily. Their skin is smooth and sensitive, but often bears a number of scars from encounters with other dolphins, sea objects, or boats. Under the dolphin's skin is a layer of blubber—a fatty substance that stores energy and helps dolphins to stay warm.

Dolphins hold their breath underwater and at the surface exhale through the blowhole, which shoots a spray of water into the air. They then inhale quickly, submerge again, and swim on.

SPECIAL FEATURES

Many other dolphin parts seem specially designed to help them live their active underwater lives. The **rostrum** is the beaklike structure that includes a dolphin's jaw and teeth. Dolphins' teeth are not meant for chewing their food. Rather their teeth allow dolphins to grasp their prey in their powerful jaws so that the captured food cannot swim away.

Dolphins' eyes have special features that enable them to see both in air and underwater. The pupils of the eyes

Dolphins' teeth help them to grip slippery fish so that their meal does not swim away.

are quite large, which permits a lot of light to enter the eyes so that dolphins can see in their dark underwater world. Muscles around the eyes can change the shape of the lenses of their eyes, allowing them to focus whether they are underwater or on the surface.

Dolphins are mammals and must breathe air to live. The blowhole is a muscular opening similar to a nostril. Dolphins inhale and exhale—breathe—through the single blowhole on the top of their heads.

Dolphins' bodies are in a fusiform shape, which means wide in the middle and narrower at each end. This helps dolphins to swim quickly and efficiently.

The curved fin on the back of a dolphin is called the dorsal fin. The dorsal fin is made up of cartilage—a strong, elastic material. Scientists believe that the dorsal fin helps give the dolphins stability as they swim through the water.

A dolphin's flukes do not have any bones or muscles. They are made of tough, fibrous tissue.

The two flippers on either side of a dolphin's body are made up of fingerlike bones surrounded by dense supportive tissue. Dolphins use their flippers while they swim in order to steer and to stop. Dolphins' tails are also important for movement. Their tails are made up of two flat, paddle-like **flukes**. When dolphins move their flukes up and down, they are propelled through the water. Flukes are made of a tough, fibrous material. The nick between the two flukes is called the median notch.

REPRODUCTION

Each species of dolphins begins to reproduce at different ages. Common dolphins start having calves—baby dolphins— when they are about four years old. Bottlenose dolphins begin to breed at about age ten for males and between five and ten years old for females. Male dolphins often compete with other males for the females' attention. Once a male and a female have mated, the pregnant female will wait about a year, depending on the dolphin species, then give birth to a single calf.

This dolphin mother and her calf will swim together for as long as six years.

Female dolphins have two mammary glands located on

their underbellies. A mother dolphin nurses her young calf with rich milk from her body for one to two years. Young dolphins stay with their mothers for up to six years.

ECHOLOCATION

Light does not travel well through water, so it can be difficult to see below the waves. Dolphins use a system called **echolocation** to be aware of what surrounds them, even when oceans and rivers are dark and murky. At the forehead of a dolphin there is a rounded fatty organ called the melon. The melon focuses sound waves into a kind of beam. When these sound waves bounce off nearby objects, a dolphin senses the reflection of the waves— how they bounce back to its melon. Based on how long it takes for the sound to return, a dolphin can tell what is nearby. This awesome natural process works much like radar.

DOLPHIN COMMUNICATION

Dolphins communicate with other dolphins vocally as well as using body language such as splashing. Some of the vocal sounds dolphins use to communicate with each other are chirps, whistles, and screams. These sounds are produced in the dolphins' nasal sacs. Dolphins use these sounds to show they are excited, scared, or happy, and to help find a member of their pod. The clicking sound dolphins produce is a feature of their echolocation system. They emit clicks to help them learn about their immediate environment, rather than to communicate with others in their dolphin pod.

When a dolphin exhales through its blowhole, it makes

These breaching—leaping—dolphins could be playing, or they could be using the sounds their splashes make to telegraph other members of their pod.

a sound called a **chuff**. Sometimes dolphins chuff more loudly as a sign of aggression. Jaw clapping occurs when a dolphin snaps its jaw shut tightly, making a clapping noise as its teeth hit together. This is used when dolphins are fighting or playing rough.

Like whales, dolphins engage in **lobtailing, spy hopping**, and **breaching**. A dolphin lobtails by smacking its tail flukes against the surface of the water. The sound produced can carry long distances in water. Dolphins may lobtail to call to other members of the pod, to warn another dolphin, or as a sign of aggression. Spy hopping occurs when a cetacean sticks its head out of the water to look around and see what is happening at the water's surface. Breaching occurs when dolphins leap out

These three members of a dolphin pod are spy hopping.

and dive back into the water with a great splash. Breaching could be used as a warning signal, but scientists also think that breaching can help members of a pod communicate where they are and in which direction they are moving. Sometimes dolphins arc in and out of the water as they swim, and they may do this in a boat's wake, running the waves made by the boat to help them gain more speed. This behavior is known as running.

SLEEP

Marine scientists still have a lot to learn about how dolphins sleep. What they do know is that dolphin sleep is very different from human sleep. Dolphins are conscious breathers, which means they have to think about taking each breath. In order to sleep and continue to breathe, it is believed that dolphins rest only half their brain at a time. While one side of the brain "sleeps," the other side is awake enough to keep the animal breathing and perhaps to stay alert to approaching danger. While they sleep, dolphins may slowly swim with a companion. If they are alone they often doze at the surface of the water.

3

Dolphins in Danger

There are many different species of dolphins. Each species has its own unique characteristics. Unfortunately, some dolphin species are endangered or even extinct. Knowing why some dolphin populations are declining is the first step in understanding how we can keep all varieties of dolphins swimming through the world's waters.

Spotted dolphins, like the one pictured here, often swim near large populations of yellowfin tuna, so they are often caught in fishnets.

HECTOR'S AND MAUI'S DOLPHINS

The Hector's dolphin and the Maui's dolphin (a sub-species of Hector's dolphin) both thrive in the coastal waters of New Zealand. Hector's dolphins live on the east coast of South Island, and Maui's dolphins live on the west coast of North Island. These are the smallest dolphins in the world. Their lifespan is about twenty years.

Both of these dolphins often get tangled in fishnets

Hector's dolphins live to be about twenty years old. Females start bearing calves when they are about nine years old, and can have a new calf every three years or so. This results in a slow population growth for Hector's dolphins.

and drown. There are only 111 Maui's dolphins surviving, and about 7,270 Hector's dolphins in the wild. The New Zealand government recently expanded the protected areas in which fisheries are not allowed to set nets that could trap Hector's and Maui's dolphins. They hope this restriction will help prevent extinction.

COMMON DOLPHIN

The common dolphin lives in most areas of the world with warm, temperate waters. Common dolphins that live near coasts have a longer beak, while those living in deeper waters have a shorter beak. These intricately patterned cetaceans grow to be about 7.5 to 8.5 feet (2.3 to 2.6 m) in length, and weigh about 300 pounds (136 kg). Common dolphins eat squid and small fish that swim in schools, such as anchovies, lantern fish, and deep-sea smelt.

As with many other types of dolphins, the biggest threat to the common dolphin is the fishnets. In addition, some cultures hunt dolphins for meat or for bait to catch other sea creatures. Common dolphin populations in the Black Sea have been seriously depleted from overhunting.

Common dolphins like this one are in danger partly because of fishing activity. The common dolphin tries to use fishing to its advantage by following fishing boats to catch fish that fall out of nets—but then get caught themselves in the nets.

BOTTLENOSE DOLPHIN

Bottlenose dolphins are among the most widespread dolphin species. These cetaceans grow to be about 12 feet (3.6 m) long and weigh some 1,250 pounds (567 kg). They live in all of the world's temperate and tropical waters. Bottlenose dolphins typically live close to a shore in harbors, bays, lagoons, estuaries, river mouths, and near beaches, where they are sometimes observed playing.

BAIJI DOLPHIN

Also called the Yangtze River dolphin or Chinese lake dolphin, the Baiji is the most critically endangered dolphin species in the world and is in fact possibly extinct. These animals live in the Yangtze River, which flows for 4,000 miles (6,437 km), dividing China into its northern and southern halves. The Baiji's habitat has changed drastically with increased development along the river. Baiji dolphins are caught in fishnets and are also killed by electric fishing, wherein electrical currents rippling through the water kill Baiji dolphins as well as the fish they prey on. They are also often injured or killed in collisions with ships' propellers. The last confirmed Baiji dolphin sighting was in 2004. A team of researchers set out in 2006 to search for signs of the species, but they found none at all, and their instruments could not detect any signs of their echolocation.

The Baiji dolphin swam the Yangtze River for perhaps thousands of years. Now, the species is thought to be extinct.

BLIND RIVER DOLPHIN

This cetacean is native to the rivers in Bangladesh, Pakistan, India, and Nepal. Currently, there are about 935 individual blind river dolphins surviving in these rivers. The population has been declining, largely because dams built to control the flow of water have separated pods of dolphins. These dams also threaten the fish that the dolphins feed on. Like other species, blind river dolphins are vulnerable to fishnet entrapment.

As their name indicates, blind river dolphins have very poor eyesight. This makes it especially difficult for them to navigate around boats, and many dolphins have been killed in collisions with propellers. Pollution and hunting also contribute to the specie's decline. Blind river dolphins are sometimes hunted to extract oil from their blubber to use as bait for catching fish. Some indigenous populations hunt this dolphin for meat.

SPOTTED DOLPHINS

Spotted dolphins are named for the patchy spots of color on their bodies. These mammals live in warm waters throughout the world. The length of the spotted dolphin is about 7 feet (2.1 m) and they weigh around 220 pounds (100 kg). This is one of the most abundant dolphin species in the world, with an estimated population of more than 3 million, although, in the 1950s there were more than 7 million of them. That is a dramatic decline in a relatively short span of time. They are a species effected very gravely by fishing.

AT RISK

While the connection between humans and dolphins is often magical, humans can also be dolphins' greatest

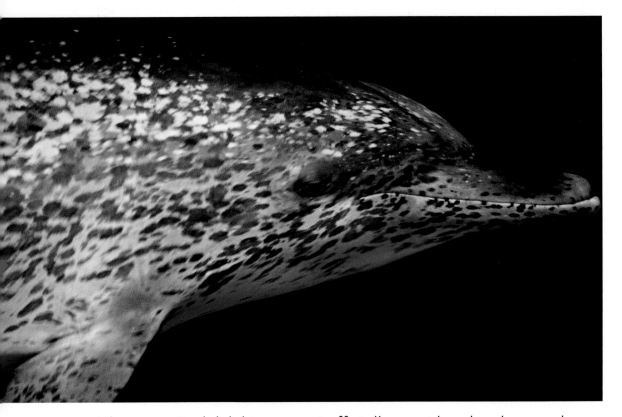

Atlantic spotted dolphins are not officially considered endangered, because there is not enough information about how many of their kind remain or how fast their numbers are declining.

threat. Fishing, pollution, other forms of habitat disruption, and even simple curiosity can lead to declining numbers of dolphins.

FISHING

The fishing industry has contributed to the decline in some dolphin populations. When fisheries gather their catch in nets, sometimes other marine life gets caught in the nets as well. Such marine life caught in nets unintentionally is called **bycatch**.

Among the biggest offenders are tuna fisheries. Tuna often swim just below pods of dolphins. Fishermen look for pods of dolphins, knowing that a good tuna catch may lie just under those dolphins. They use a net technique called purse-seine fishing to catch the tuna. In this form of fishing, a large net is cast out with weights on one end and floaters on the other end. (Imagine a fence rising from deep in the water up to the surface.) As soon as this net is cast out, the boat drives in a large circle around a school of fish. Once the school is surrounded, fishermen pull a rope that closes the bottom of the net—the "purse" part with weights on it. In the case of tuna, when fishermen haul it in, they have a full net of tuna but also could have dolphins in the net. Because spotted dolphins often swim where tuna swim, they are a common bycatch in purse-seine fishing.

Another threat to dolphins is simply collisions between dolphins and the propellers of seacraft. No one knows

From giant commercial ships like the one here to ordinary pleasure boats, traffic on the seaways is a major peril to dolphins and other marine life.

exactly how many dolphins are killed or injured this way each year. Scientists are concerned that increasing ship traffic will lead to more dolphin injuries and deaths.

HABITAT DISRUPTION

Sometimes dolphins are harmed indirectly when the places they live are polluted or changed in ways that have a negative impact on marine life. Water development projects can cause major changes to a dolphin's habitat. A major threat is the construction of new dams. When a river is dammed, a wall cuts off the flow of water. River dolphins are effected when their habitat is altered with dams. Often a new dam separates pod members into smaller groups. These different segments of the pod can no longer swim together. Because there are fewer dolphins to choose to mate with, dolphin calves are not as diverse. Diversity is an important part of the survival of any species. Dams also affect the mating and migration of other river life, including the fish that dolphins eat. Less food also leads to hardship for river dolphins.

Climate change is the warming of the earth's temperature and it impacts all species in some way, including dolphins. Certain cetaceans need to live in cold water. As waters warm up, their natural habitat gets changed, and if they cannot adapt to such changes quickly enough, they become vulnerable. Climate change can also affect how much food is available for dolphins.

Noise pollution can be a major problem for marine

mammals that rely on echolocation and hearing in order to communicate and navigate. Noise travels long distances under water. When naval ships use sonar, they may be interfering with marine mammal activity. Other sources of noise pollution include searching and drilling for oil and running boat engines. When cetaceans are faced with a noisy habitat, scientists believe it is more difficult for them to find food, to communicate with other members of the pod, and to reproduce.

CONTROVERSY AT MARINE PARKS

Throughout the United States and other parts of the world some marine parks and other programs put on shows in which dolphins do "tricks" or offer people the opportunity to swim with dolphins. **Conservation** groups are at work to ban these programs. Organizations such as the Humane Society of the United States argue that the conditions captive dolphins must endure are unnatural and punishing. They believe that no marine park has an adequate setup to allow dolphins, who can swim up to 100 miles (161 km) per day, the freedom they enjoy in the

Do you think dolphins in marine parks actually help to educate the public, or do they contribute to the decline of dolphins?

wild. The Humane Society also argues that dolphin petting and feeding encounters are dangerous for dolphins' health, and humans' safety.

Fortunately, there are people working throughout the world to counteract these exposures and advance the conservation of dolphins.

4

Saving Dolphins

With their playful demeanor and the affinity dolphins show with humans, people around the world want to conserve dolphins and help in making their habitats safe from fishnets, pollution, and other dangers. Sadly, some species of dolphins may already be gone for good, though acting now will help to keep other species safe from going the same way.

Dolphins face many dangers in the wild, from fishnets and ship propellers to pollution and habitat destruction.

CONSERVATION GROUPS

Some devoted organizations are working very hard to educate people about the dangers dolphins face and to reduce the number and severity of threatening conditions. The World Wildlife Fund (WWF) works in more than one hundred countries across the globe to protect endangered dolphin populations and other threatened species. The Whale and Dolphin Conservation Society is also hard at work protecting cetaceans. They campaign

A captive dolphin curiously approaches this painter.

to reduce threats such as hunting, pollution, and net entrapment. They also raise money to support scientific research into cetaceans and the ways to conserve them.

LAWS PROTECTING DOLPHINS

In the United States, and in many other concerned countries in the world, governments enact laws that will help protect dolphins and other endangered or threatened species. The Endangered Species Act of 1973 is one of the most important U.S. laws passed for threatened cetaceans and other animal species. Under this law, if a species is listed as endangered or threatened, it is illegal to injure, kill, sell, carry, deliver, or possess any such animal. The punishment is a fine of up to $50,000 and possibly time in jail. It also makes it illegal to destroy the habitat of an endangered species.

The Marine Mammal Protection Act was passed by Congress in 1972, making it illegal to catch marine mammals—including dolphins, whales, porpoises, seals, and sea lions—from U.S. waters. It is also illegal for American citizens to take marine mammals from any waters in the

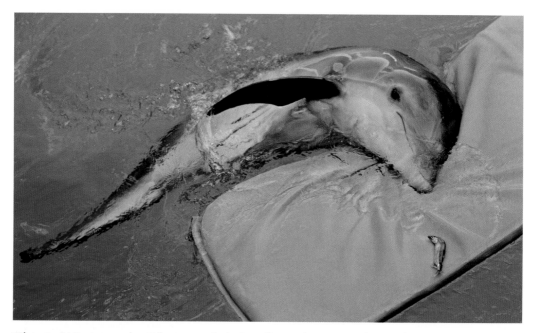

This is Winter, a bottlenose dolphin found trapped in a fishing line in Florida. She was rescued, but her tail could not be saved. Here, she receives care and rehabilitation at the Clearwater Marine Aquarium.

world, or to import them or products—such as fertilizer and machine lubricants—made from them.

The Agreement on the International Dolphin Conservation Program (AIDCP) aims to prevent dolphin bycatch in tuna fishing. Costa Rica, Ecuador, El Salvador, Guatemala, Honduras, Mexico, Nicaragua, Panama, Peru, the United States, Vanuatu, and Venezuela have each officially ratified—or made into law—the agreement.

SAFER FISHING

Many tuna fisheries have changed the way they fish for tuna, trying to be more careful not to capture dolphins as bycatch. Consumers who want to buy tuna from a company that does not harm dolphins can look for a dolphin-safe logo on the tuna cans they buy in the store. In order to merit the United States Department of Commerce dolphin-safe logo, fishing fleets in the eastern tropical Pacific Ocean must not target pods of dolphins in their search for tuna. An observer from the National Marine Fisheries Service is aboard each fishing boat to make sure the rule is followed. The Earth Island Institute and EarthTrust, both conservation groups, award their own dolphin-safe logos as well.

Consumers who want to make sure that dolphins were not harmed in fishing practices can look for the "dolphin-safe" logo on products like canned tuna.

FIGHTING POLLUTION

As scientists have recognized the dangers of fertilizers entering water systems, government legislation has banned or limited the use of these and other dangerous chemicals. Even pollution like litter can have devastating effects on individual dolphins. Stray pieces of fishing line can wrap around dolphins' flippers or tails, causing great pain and damage. It can cause a dolphin to lose part of its tail or one of its flippers. If a dolphin swallows trash such as soda can rings, it can choke or cause internal damage. Being more careful about recycling materials and properly disposing of garbage can help to save marine life.

WHAT YOU CAN DO

No matter where you live, you can play a part in protecting threatened and endangered dolphins. You can write to the lawmakers in your state, asking them to support laws that will protect dolphins and the environment. Avoid releasing balloons! When balloons float aloft, they can drift far away and wind up in rivers and oceans. Marine mammals may swallow the balloons while eating,

These demonstrators are doing their part to educate the public about dolphin conservation.

which can make them very sick. Recycle to conserve all of our world's natural resources and prevent trash from polluting our oceans and rivers. Boycott products or services that can cause harm to dolphins. For example, buy only dolphin-safe tuna. If you visit marine parks, do not feed the dolphins or pet them, even if it is offered by the park. Ask the marine park staff members not to exhibit wild-caught dolphins.

What will the future bring for dolphins? No one knows for sure. But you, together with other **conservationists**, can help shape that future by working now to protect dolphins and their habitats.

GLOSSARY

blowhole—A muscular opening on the top of a dolphin's head, through which it exhales and inhales.

breaching—When a cetacean leaps out of the water and reenters it with a great splash.

bycatch—Marine life unintentionally caught in nets cast by fishers.

calf—A baby dolphin.

cetacean—An animal that belongs to the scientific order Cetacea, which includes marine mammals, such as dolphins, whales, and porpoises.

chuff—The sound made when a dolphin exhales through its blow-hole.

conservation—Working to help wild animals and plants to survive.

conservationists—People who work to save threatened and endangered species.

echolocation—A system of being aware of surroundings by giving off a series of clicks and analyzing the reflection of sound waves.

endangered—Being in danger of disappearing forever.

flukes—Making up the tail, the twin flukes are flat and paddle like, and are moved up and down to propel a dolphin through water.

habitat—The type of environment in which an animals lives.

lobtail—When a dolphin smacks its tail flukes against the surface of the water to call to other members of the pod, to warn another dolphin, or as a sign of aggression.

pod—A group of dolphins that swims together, usually with twelve to twenty-four members.

porpoise—A type of cetacean that resembles a dolphin, but is a different species.

rostrum—The beak-like structure making up a dolphin's jaw and teeth.

species—A specific type of animal. For example, bottlenose dolphins are a species of dolphin.

spy hopping—When a cetacean sticks its head out of the water to look around and see what is happening at the water's surface.

superpod—A group of several pods swimming together in a larger group of hundreds or even thousands of dolphins.

FIND OUT MORE

Books

Crisp, Marty. *Everything Dolphin: What Kids Really Want to Know about Dolphins.* Minnetonka, MN: NorthWord Books for Young Readers. 2004.

Nicklin, Flip, and Linda Nicklin. *Face to Face with Dolphins.* Des Moines, IA: National Geographic Children's Books. 2007.

Rhodes, Mary Jo, and David Hall. *Dolphins, Seals, and Other Sea Mammals.* Danbury, CT: Children's Press. 2007.

Web Sites

National Geographic Kids Bottlenose Dolphin Page
http://kids.nationalgeographic.com/Animals/CreatureFeature/
   Bottlenose-dolphin

WWF Endangered Cetaceans
http://www.panda.org/what_we_do/endangered_species/cetaceans/

World Society for the Protection of Animals—Dolphin Facts
http://www.wspa-usa.org/pages/2222_dolphin_facts_for_kids.cfm

INDEX

Pages numbers in **boldface** are illustrations.

ABOUT THE AUTHOR

Johannah Haney has written books about whales, seals, and many other topics for Marshall Cavendish Benchmark. She lives in Boston, where she received her master's degree in writing and publishing. She has stood just a few yards away from a chuffing bottlenose dolphin and her baby in the Caloosahatchee River in Fort Myers, Florida.